This book belongs to:

CONNOR
_____

TO MY LITTLE BASKETBALL PLAYER.
I LOVE SHOOTING BASKETS WITH Y   IOT.
I LOVE YOU !!

GRANDPA

FOR MY HOMETOWN & MY FIRSTBORN

Hurley, Mississippi and Dean McCoy
both taught me about hard work, courage,
and doing things my own way.

All illustrations in this book were created by hand using watercolor,
acrylic, pencil, ink, and digital magic. Some wording is hand-lettered
by Melissa Smith Turner. No part of this book may be reproduced,
transmitted, copied, or stored without permission from the publisher.

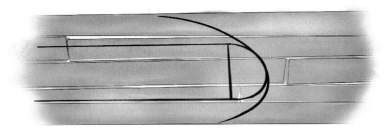

ISBN: 9798644799749
Imprint: Independently published

Created & Printed in the U.S.A.

My name is Hurley McCoy.

Once upon a time,
I was a **plain,**

boring,

just okay

basketball dribbler.

Anybody can be **plain and boring**.
I wanted to be a better, **super,
big time** basketball dribbler.

I wanted to be
dynamite!

So, this is the story of how

I, **Hurley McCoy,**
became a super great

dynamite
dribbler!

Before I was dynamite . . .

**I could hold
the ball.**

(Babies can do that.)

**I could bounce
and catch.**

(Easy.)

**I could roll the
ball on the
ground.**

(Boring.)

**I could hold the ball
above my head.**

(Very boring.)

Everyone knows, the best way to become **dynamite** at anything **is** PRACTiCE

And that's exactly what I did.
I practiced a lot.

I started by dribbling up and down, **up and down**, with each hand.

I dribbled up and down so many times, I started to feel the Earth shake.

I made sure to keep
my wrist **strong**.

Dynamite dribblers
don't slap the ball,
**they push
the ball.**

Next, I wanted to be **even more dynamite.**

I learned how to run and dribble at the same time.

I kept my eyes looking forward so I wouldn't run into anything and look like a **clumsy ostrich!**

Then, I learned to stop my foot very fast. This is called a **jab step**, and it is a very dynamite skill.

I also became a master at dribbling from one hand to the other. This is called a **crossover**.

The skill that takes the most work is dribbling **between my legs.**

I bounce the ball under my legs and catch it on the back side.

This is a very hard skill, and sometimes the ball just rolls away instead of me catching it.

I will keep working on that one.

Finally,

I got to put all my dynamite dribbling skills together **and** use them in a

real basketball game!

When the ball was passed to me,
I dribbled and ran.

I kept my eyes forward while
pushing the ball
up and down.

When someone on
the other team
tried to steal

the ball . . .

I tricked him with a
jab step
and a
crossover.

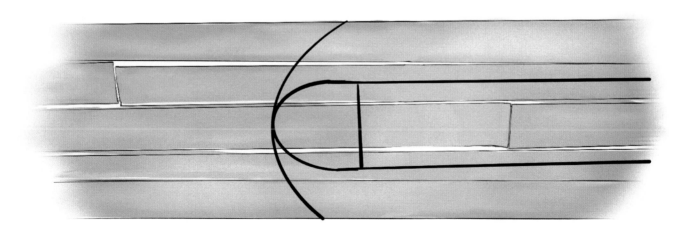

Then, a quick
dribble under the legs
and pass to my
open teammate . . .

**The shot goes
in the net . . .**

After the game,

everyone

said . . .

. . . "Hurley McCoy,
you are a
**dynamite
dribbler!"**

Dynamite Skills
Skills
Checklist:

☐ DRIBBLE WITH RIGHT HAND

☐ HOLD THE BALL

☐ DRIBBLE WITH LEFT HAND

☐ BOUNCE AND CATCH

☐ WALK AND DRIBBLE

☐ ROLL THE BALL

☐ RUN AND DRIBBLE

☐ HOLD THE BALL
ABOVE YOUR HEAD

☐ JAB STEP

- [ ] CROSSOVER

- [ ] DRIBBLE BETWEEN LEGS

- [ ] PASS THE BALL

- [ ] CATCH A PASS

- [ ] SHOOT THE BALL

- [ ] MAKE A SHOT

What else can you do?

_____

_____

_____

_____

_____

_____

Melissa Smith Turner is an artist who likes drawing pictures and telling stories. She started out writing simple little funny tales for her own five children. Now, she shares her stories with readers all over the world. She is also the author & illustrator of the popular Alma Louise children's book series.

Melissa is not a dynamite basketball dribbler, but she is married to a guy named Charlie who is. She also knows two sports experts named Dean and Hal who gave her lots of advice and inspiration for this book.

Made in the USA
Monee, IL
01 August 2020